The New Girl

by Laurie Calkhoven

illustrated by Arcana Studios

American Girl®

Questions or comments? Call 1-800-845-0005,
visit americangirl.com, or write to Customer Service,
American Girl, 8400 Fairway Place, Middleton, WI 53562-0497.

Printed in China
12 13 14 15 16 17 LEO 10 9 8 7 6 5 4 3 2 1

Illustrated by Thu Thai at Arcana Studios

Welcome to Innerstar University! At this imaginary, one-of-a-kind school, you can live with your friends in a dorm called Brightstar House and find lots of fun ways to let your true talents shine. Your friends at Innerstar U will help you find your way through some challenging situations, too.

When you reach a page in this book that asks you to make a decision, choose carefully. The decisions you make will lead to more than 20 different endings! (*Hint:* Use a pencil to check off your choices. That way, you'll never read the same story twice.)

Want to try another ending? Read the book again—and then again. Find out what would have happened if you'd made *different* choices. Then head to www.innerstarU.com for even more book endings, games, and fun with friends.

Innerstar Guides

Every girl needs a few good friends to help her find her way. These are the friends who are always there for **you**.

Emmy
A brave girl who loves swimming and boating

Isabel
A confident girl with a funky sense of style

Riley
A good sport, on the field and off

Paige
A nature lover who leads hikes and campus cleanups

Amber

An animal lover and
a loyal friend

Neely

A creative girl who loves
dance, music, and art

Logan

A super-smart girl
who is curious about
EVERYTHING

Shelby

A kind girl who is there
for her friends—and loves
making NEW friends!

Innerstar U Campus

1. Rising Star Stables
2. Star Student Center
3. Brightstar House
4. Starlight Library
5. Sparkle Studios
6. Blue Sky Nature Center

7. Real Spirit Center
8. Five-Points Plaza
9. Starfire Lake & Boathouse
10. U-Shine Hall
11. Good Sports Center
12. Shopping Square
13. The Market
14. Morningstar Meadow

ou leave your last class of the day and start planning your afternoon. There's so much to do at Innerstar University that sometimes it's hard to choose. Hanging out with your friends? Horseback riding? A yoga class?

Hanging out with your friends wins, so you head toward Brightstar House. You're about to knock on your friend Shelby's door when it pops open.

Shelby greets you with a happy grin. "I have great news!" she says.

Shelby's practically dancing with excitement. When she has good news, she can't wait to share it.

"There's a new girl coming to school tomorrow," says Shelby. "Her name is Zoé, and she's from *France*."

 Turn to page 10.

Shelby shows you a picture of a pretty dark-haired girl with a friendly smile. "Wow," you say, "all the way from France?"

"Yes!" says Shelby. "Just for the semester, but it'll be fun to get to know her."

You're not surprised that Shelby is excited to meet Zoé. Shelby was one of your first friends at Innerstar U, and she made you feel right at home. You can be nervous when it comes to meeting new people and trying new things, but Shelby never shies away from making new friends.

Isabel pops up from behind Shelby, her blue eyes sparkling. "Zoé can tell us all about Paris fashions!" she says happily. "Style and sophistication. Ooh la la!"

Isabel has a great, funky style all her own. She's the go-to girl when you need a shopping buddy or an honest opinion on an outfit. Isabel will find plenty of things to talk about with Zoé, but will you?

Turn to page 12.

Schoo

Graduatior
Perso

2nd

"Let's plan a party to make Zoé feel welcome," Shelby suggests. "Maybe we can do pizza at the Party Place."

A party? You were the new girl at Innerstar U not too long ago, and you don't remember anyone throwing *you* a party. Now your fear about meeting the new girl has an added twist—you're a little jealous.

"A party is a great idea!" Isabel says. "I'll handle the invitations."

"I've got the food covered," Shelby says.

You're not sure you'll have time to help plan a party for Zoé. Plus, you're nervous about meeting her. You've never known anyone from France, and you're afraid you and Zoé won't have anything in common. What do you do?

 If you help plan Zoé's welcome party, turn to page 14.

 If you bow out of party planning, turn to page 16.

You help Logan and Neely hang their posters while they tell you all about the Innerstar U Games.

"The student council runs them every year," Logan says. "Teams compete in all kinds of events, like funny sports and puzzle solving."

"It's totally wacky," Neely says.

"The teams earn stars for every challenge," Logan explains. "And the two teams that earn the most points have a showdown at the end."

"Sounds like fun!" you say. "Can I be on your team?"

Logan shakes her head. "Teams are picked at random," she says. "That's part of the fun—new friends!"

"Want to sign up?" Neely asks.

You hesitate. You don't want to admit that you're a little afraid to sign up, especially if you might end up on a team with girls you don't know. What if you make a fool of yourself in one of those wacky challenges?

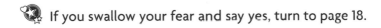 If you swallow your fear and say yes, turn to page 18.

 If you decide to sit out the games this year, turn to page 23.

"You've got the food and the invitations covered," you say to your friends. "How about if I make a welcome sign for Zoé's door?"

"Great idea!" Shelby says.

You're on your way to Sparkle Studios when you spot Logan and Neely coming toward you, carrying stacks of papers. A gust of wind pulls a few papers right out of Neely's hands and scatters them in all directions. One is teetering on the edge of the stream that feeds Starfire Lake.

"Oh, no," Neely squeals. "My posters!" She's weighed down with other posters, and so is Logan.

"I'll get them," you say, chasing after the poster nearest to you.

Turn to page 17.

"Sorry," you tell Shelby and Isabel. "I can't help with the party. I've got a *ton* of homework."

Shelby is understanding, as always. "No problem," she says. "We've got the party covered. But you'll still be there to welcome Zoé, right?"

"I'll try," you say with a tight smile. "Right now, I've got to hit the books."

At dinner that night, you get a nervous feeling in your stomach every time you hear Zoé's name. The more excited your friends seem to be about meeting Zoé, the more nervous you become.

By the time you get back to your room that night, you've decided to skip the party. You're convinced that if you went, you'd only fumble for conversation with Zoé and make a total fool of yourself.

Turn to page 19.

You catch up to Neely's poster just before it drops into the water, and then you grab the others. "Got 'em!" you yell.

You check out one of the posters as you carry them back to Neely. It says:

Want to get wild and wacky?
Want to make new friends?
Want to win fun prizes?
Sign up for this year's Innerstar U Games!

"Thanks," Neely says when you hand over the posters. "I worked hard on those and didn't want to start all over again. We're going to hang them up around campus."

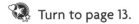 Turn to page 13.

You brush your nervousness aside. The games sound like too much fun to pass up. If everyone's doing the same crazy stunts, what's there to be embarrassed about? And like Logan said, making new friends will be part of the fun.

You borrow Neely's pink marker and write your name on the sign-up sheet in big letters. Then you help Logan and Neely hang their last poster before heading to Sparkle Studios to make Zoé's welcome sign.

An hour later, you hang the sign on the door of Zoé's new room at Brightstar House. You hope the sign is stylish and sophisticated enough for a girl from France.

Then you knock on Shelby's door to tell her your own good news—you've signed up for the games!

 Turn to page 22.

The next night, Shelby stops by to find out how your studying is going and to tell you about Zoé. "She's really sweet, but she's nervous about coming to a new school," Shelby says. "I remember how scared I was on my first day, too."

"You—scared?" you ask. "But you're so good at making friends."

"I didn't used to be," Shelby explains. "I was way too nervous. But I learned a good trick for fighting nervousness: I just try to make the other person feel like we're old friends, and it seems to help me, too. That—and asking a lot of questions!"

You think about Shelby's trick. Maybe if you treated Zoé like a friend instead of hiding out in your room, you could help her feel at home—and help yourself feel less nervous. And since you don't know very much about France, you certainly have lots of questions you could ask her.

"Is Zoé in her room now?" you ask. "I want to introduce myself—and ask her some questions about France!"

By the time Zoé answers your knock on her door, you're already smiling. *"Bonjour,"* you say, using the French word for hello. "Welcome to Innerstar U. I hope we're going to be great friends."

When you see Zoé's smile and hear her shy "hello," you're pretty sure that you *will* be.

The End

The next afternoon, you and your friends wait for Zoé in the lobby of Brightstar House. Your friends are *so* excited. You should be, too, but for some reason, you can't shake this nagging feeling of jealousy.

When Shelby finally leads Zoé through the front door and into the lobby, you're struck by how nervous she looks. You were pretty scared the first time you walked into Brightstar House, wondering if you would fit in. *It must be even scarier when you're from another country,* you think.

"Hello. *Bonjour,*" Zoé says shyly. She gives each of you a kiss—on both cheeks.

Isabel giggles. "I like the way the French say hello," she says.

You all lead Zoé to her room, and Shelby tells her about the party at six o'clock. You invite Zoé to knock on your door when she's ready to go. Walking to the party together will give you a chance to get to know her better, and once you do, you're sure this jealousy thing will pass.

"*Oui, merci,*" Zoé says to you. Then she laughs, shakes her head, and says, "I mean, yes, *thank you.*"

A couple of hours later, you wait for Zoé's knock, but it doesn't come. Five minutes after the party was supposed to start, you knock on her door. There's no answer.

If you head to the party without her, turn to page 26.

If you wait for a while and knock again, turn to page 31.

Shelby is hanging out in her room with Logan, Neely, and Isabel. Logan is reading about France on the Internet, and Neely and Shelby are helping Isabel finish the party invitations.

You don't waste any time telling your friends that you signed up for the games. It's really big news for you, but for some reason, they don't seem quite as excited about it as you are.

"That's cool," Shelby says. "I'll be taking pictures of the games for the yearbook."

"I had a blast last year," Isabel adds.

"I hope we'll end up on the same team!" you say.

But Isabel has already starting talking about the new girl again. "I'll bet Zoé is really glamorous," she says.

"And has a great French accent," Neely adds.

That jealous feeling pops up again. If the new girl is all anyone can talk about now, what will it be like after she actually arrives at school?

 Turn to page 20.

You think it's better to sit out the games than to risk embarrassing yourself. "I have too much schoolwork," you fib to your friends. You head to Sparkle Studios to make Zoé's welcome sign, not giving the games another thought.

But soon, the whole campus is buzzing about the games, and you feel a little left out. Over lunch with Shelby one day, you say, "I'm mad at myself for missing all the fun."

"Being mad at yourself won't help," Shelby says. "Trying new things can be scary, but sometimes you have to be brave and go for it. Why don't we stop by the student council office and see if any of the teams still need a member? Or you can help me—I'm taking pictures for the yearbook, and I could use another photographer."

Butterflies fill your stomach, but this time you're going to be brave.

 If you agree to help Shelby, turn to page 38.

 If you head to the student council office, turn to page 28.

Logan's invitation catches you off guard. "But I thought you only wanted to spend time with Zoé," you say.

Logan's jaw drops. "That's not true!" she says.

Shelby gives you a hug. "I *always* make a fuss about new girls, to make them feel at home," she says. "But that doesn't mean I don't have time for my old friends."

Now you're a little embarrassed. "Sorry, guys," you say.

"Don't be sorry," says Shelby. "It's brave to speak up and say what you feel. I'm glad you did."

You wish you had been brave enough to talk to your friends sooner. And you're sorry you didn't do more to reach out to Zoé. But maybe you can still fix that.

"Hanging out tonight would be great," you tell your friends. "But let's see if Zoé wants to join us, too."

The End

It's brave to speak up and say what you feel.

You go back to your room and close your door. You felt a little hurt yesterday when news of Zoé's arrival seemed so much more important to your friends than your own news about the games. That wasn't Zoé's fault, of course, but leaving you hanging like this is.

You could go to the party and ask her what happened, but you're not really in a party mood anymore.

You try to focus on homework, but it's hard. It's okay if Zoé doesn't want to be friends with you, but what about Shelby and the others? It hurts that no one has noticed that you're not at the party.

You've barely finished that thought when there's a knock on your door. You open it to find Shelby and Zoé. Before you can speak, Zoé apologizes.

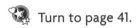 Turn to page 41.

You're just leaving Brightstar House when you spot Isabel and Zoé running toward you. They're carrying bags from Dream Décor and Casual Closet, and they're both wearing berry-colored berets.

You feel left out and forgotten—again. Why didn't they invite you to go shopping? You try to push the feeling aside.

"Bonjour!" Zoé says breathlessly. "Isabel's been helping me find things to dress up my room."

"And Zoé's been helping me find things to dress *me* up!" Isabel says.

Zoé checks her watch. "In France we use the 24-hour clock," she says. "I thought the party was at 16:00—or four o'clock. I looked for you then, but you weren't in your room."

"She found me and I explained that the party was at six," Isabel said. "Zoé wanted to check out the Shopping Square. We came across a great sale. I guess we lost track of time."

 Turn to page 30.

Shelby's support gives you courage. You walk to the student council office together and discover that one of the members of the Shining Stars team sprained her ankle and had to drop out. "Do you want to join?" a council member asks you.

You take a look at the list of girls on the team. You're friends with two of them, Paige and Riley. But you don't know the other two girls—Sophie and Cassie—at all. That makes you a little nervous, but this time, you're not going to let your nerves stop you.

You agree to join the team, and before you know it, you're surrounded by your new teammates, decorating T-shirts and painting a banner for the opening ceremonies. The next day, the Shining Stars are headed for their first event!

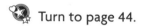 Turn to page 44.

Midway through the games, you and Shelby meet in the yearbook office to look over your pictures.

"These are great shots," Shelby says, pointing to pictures of the watermelon relay race. You've also got fun photos of the determined look on Zoé's face during the tug-of-war—and her surprised expression when she lands in the muddy pit a second later.

At the final challenge, when it's down to just two teams, the Good Sports Center is full of girls cheering on their friends. Taking pictures is super exciting. You're in the middle of all the action, which you figure is the next best thing to competing.

Next year, though, maybe you'll be brave enough to actually join a team. *Wild and wacky*, you think. *Bring it on!*

The End

You feel better now that you know Zoé didn't leave you hanging on purpose, but you still feel a little left out.

"It looks like it was a successful shopping trip," you say, pointing to Zoé's and Isabel's bags. "You both look so cute in those berets."

Isabel laughs and strikes a pose. "Do I look Parisian?" she asks.

"Totally," you tell her, giggling. "Can I see the rest of your bargains?"

Zoé starts to open one of her shopping bags, but Isabel checks her watch and shakes her head. "I don't think there's enough time," she says. "Would you mind going to Party Place and letting them know we're on our way? We just have to take these bags upstairs. I'll get Zoé over to the party."

Zoé gives you an apologetic shrug as she gathers up her bags.

"No problem," you say, forcing a smile. "I'll see you over there."

 Turn to page 32.

You leave your door open in case Zoé walks by. Fifteen minutes later, you knock again on the door of her room. Still no answer.

You know the others went to the student center early to decorate for the party. Could Zoé have gone with them without telling you? That would be kind of rude.

You also know that when people fly long distances across different time zones, it can be hard to adjust to the new time. Could Zoé have jet lag and be asleep?

You hate the idea of her missing her own party. What should you do?

 If you open Zoé's door, turn to page 35.

If you head over to Party Place to see if she's there, turn to page 26.

On your way over to the student center, you try to shake off your hurt feelings. But as soon as you walk into the party room, your jealousy kicks in again.

"Where's Zoé?" Logan asks, without even saying hi. "We thought she'd be with you."

"The pizza's getting cold," someone else says with a groan. "And I'm hungry."

You explain what happened, and a few minutes later, Isabel and Zoé rush into the room. All the girls gather around to meet Zoé and to ask her questions about her life in France. With Zoé in the room, you feel totally invisible.

When Neely says Zoé signed up for the Innerstar U Games, everyone cheers.

"I hope we're on the same team," Isabel says to Zoé.

"Me, too!" Logan adds.

Your friends sure weren't this excited when you told them *you* signed up for the games. *No one seems to care whether I join the games, but they all want to be on Zoé's team,* you think sadly. You're not sure how much more of this you can take.

If you decide to drop out of the games, turn to page 34.

If you decide to drop out of the games, turn to page 34.

If you decide to make the best of it, turn to page 36.

As soon as you can, you slip out of the party. You head straight to the Innerstar U Games sign-up sheet and cross your name off the list.

The next day, Logan asks you why you dropped out of the games.

You shrug. "I'm just really busy with classes," you fib.

Logan cocks her head to the side and studies your face. "Are you sure that's all?" she asks. "You seem upset about something."

You think about telling Logan how you feel, but instead, you simply shake your head. You're afraid that if you talk about your fears, you'll find out that they're true—that now that Zoé's arrived, no one cares if you're around or not.

You don't talk to Logan again until the first day of the Innerstar U Games. Everyone but you seems to be taking part in the opening ceremony—and having a blast. You feel totally left out. You try to cheer on the teams, but it's hard.

After the final event of the day, you're on your way back to Brightstar House. You hear footsteps behind you, and you turn to find Logan and Shelby racing to catch up with you, still wearing their team T-shirts.

"Want to hang out tonight?" Logan asks, stopping to catch her breath. "We've been so busy with the games that it feels like we haven't seen you in ages. We've missed you!"

 Turn to page 24.

You don't want to invade anyone's privacy, but you don't want Zoé to miss her own party. You turn her doorknob to see if the door is unlocked, and it is. You tiptoe into the room.

It looks empty, but you can't see the bedroom loft from where you are. You climb the stairs to check Zoé's bed. There's an open suitcase on the bed, but no Zoé.

It looks as if she's left already, which kind of annoys you—especially after you were reaching out to her in friendship.

 If you decide to skip Zoé's party entirely, turn to page 25.

 If you head over to Party Place, turn to page 26.

You wake up the next morning determined to make the best of whatever happens. *Of course* your friends are going to make a big fuss about Zoé. She was really brave to come to a new school in a new country, and everyone wants to make her feel at home.

Teams for the Innerstar U Games are being announced today, and you're excited to find out who else is on your team. You decide to knock on Zoé's door to see if she wants to walk over to the student center with you. As you step out into the hall, you see that Logan is already standing there in front of Zoé's door.

"Hi," she says. "I think Zoé left already. I need someone to help me draw names for the teams. Would you like to do it?"

"Um, sure," you say with a smile. But what you're really thinking is that you're Logan's *second* choice—after Zoé.

The student center is full of girls excited about the games. Logan explains how choosing the teams is going to work. For each team, you'll pull five names out of a hat, and Logan will announce them.

As you hand names to Logan and she calls them out, you watch girls introducing themselves to new teammates. Every once in a while a girl lets out a loud cheer when she ends up on a team with a good friend.

One of those cheers comes from Isabel when Logan calls her name, immediately after Zoé's. They're on the same team as Jamie and Becca, a couple of girls you know pretty well.

You reach into the hat to pull out the fifth name, and you recognize the bright pink marker through the folded paper. It's *you*.

You're not sure you want to be on a team with Zoé. Will that mean you'll keep coming in second?

If you drop your name and choose another one, turn to page 40.

If you hand your name over to Logan, turn to page 42.

During the opening ceremony at the Good Sports Center, you and Shelby run around taking shots of all the teams. They've chosen wacky team names and splashed them across banners and T-shirts.

As each team is announced, the team members head into the stadium doing different tricks. Neely's team plays leapfrog. Zoé's team cartwheels in.

You get better and better at snapping pictures at *just* the right moment.

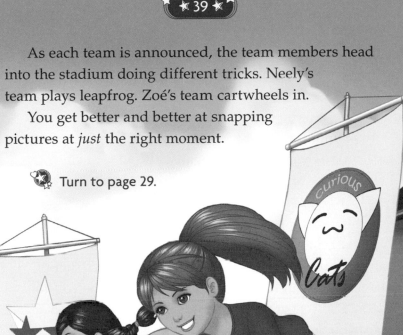

Turn to page 29.

You drop your name and fish another one out of the hat, telling yourself that you're doing it because you'd really like to be on a team with Logan and Shelby. The truth is, you don't want to keep coming in second to Zoé.

You hand the folded piece of paper to Logan, and your heart sinks when the name Logan calls out is Shelby's. Now Shelby will be on *Zoé's* team, not yours.

Isabel gives Shelby a big high five. "We can name our team the Fashionistas!" she announces.

A few minutes later, you pull your name out of the hat again, and this time you hand it to Logan. You're happy to be teamed with Paige and Riley, two girls you consider friends. They cheer when your name is called, and that makes you feel good.

Two girls you don't know at all—Sophie and Cassie— round out your team.

 Turn to page 43.

"I am so sorry," she says in her French accent. "I forgot to ask your room number. I wandered through the dorm, but it seemed like everyone was already gone, so I used my campus map to find the student center."

"I was coming over to get you," Shelby explains, "but I got pulled into the yearbook office to answer a question, and it took forever. Zoé came out in search of both of us!"

You're embarrassed now, thinking about how hurt you felt over such a silly mistake. If you had just gone to the party and asked Zoé what happened, you would have saved yourself a lot of heartache.

The three of you walk to the party arm in arm. *Next time*, you promise yourself, *I'll be brave enough to ask my friends what's going on* before *I jump to crazy conclusions!*

The End

You're nervous about being on Zoé's team, but picking another name feels like cheating. You take a deep breath and hand the piece of paper over to Logan.

When Logan calls out your name, Isabel cheers and waves at you. That makes you feel good. You wave back with a big smile on your face, but Isabel doesn't see you—she has already turned back to Zoé, who is standing beside her, and the two of them are talking excitedly.

You're tired of everyone making such a fuss over Zoé. Being on a team with her is going to be hard to take, but you're stuck now. What choice do you have?

After all the teams are announced, you join Isabel and your other team members to make a plan. You agree to meet at Sparkle Studios for a T-shirt–painting and strategy session.

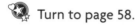 Turn to page 58.

As soon as all the teams are chosen, you and your four teammates head outside to get to know one another and to choose a team name. You settle on the "Shining Stars."

Two days later, you march into the Good Sports Center with your team, wearing matching T-shirts and waving a Shining Stars banner. The field of the sports center is filled with girls wearing T-shirts in every color of the rainbow. Banners are flying high, and so are your spirits. You're so glad you decided to join the games!

As the opening ceremony begins, the members of last year's winning team run around the track, pumping their fists in the air. A few student council members make some funny remarks. Afterward, you all shout together, "Let the wackiness begin!"

To get started, one member from each of the fifteen teams draws a number to see who gets first choice at the first challenge. You're super excited when your team asks you to represent them, and then you draw the number 1! You run up to the judges' table and check out the list of events. You want to choose one you think the Shining Stars can win.

If you choose a game called "Who Am I?" turn to page 44.

If you choose "Row, Row, Row Your Boat," turn to page 46.

The first challenge—"Who Am I?"—sounds like a thinking game. You're pretty good at thinking games, and you want to come through for your team.

You follow Paige, Riley, and the rest of your team as they run toward Morningstar Meadow. When you get there, you find yourself pitted against the Fashionistas and Logan's team, the Curious Cats. The game rules say that three of the girls on your team will wear hats. The other two won't. The hats have blank index cards tucked into the hatbands.

If you grab a hat, turn to page 52.

If you let other girls take the hats, turn to page 47.

The Shining Stars head to Starfire Lake for the "Row, Row, Row Your Boat" game. You haven't spent much time in a boat, but Paige, Riley, and Cassie are all great athletes, so you hope your team will do well.

But when you get to the lake, you realize that rowing isn't what you'll be doing. The "rowboats" are actually inflatable boats, and they're missing one essential item—oars!

Once again, the Shining Stars will compete against the Fashionistas and the Curious Cats. You strap on a lifejacket while you listen to the lifeguard explain the rules, which are simple: Make your way across the lake and back without oars. The first-place team will earn ten stars.

The girl in the back of the boat will be the team leader on this challenge. Where do you want to sit?

 If you hop in the front of the boat, turn to page 50.

 If you take the back of the boat, turn to page 48.

Paige, Cassie, and Sophie all put on hats. Then the game leader blows a whistle and tells you and Riley to turn over the cards on the hats without showing the other girls what's on them.

Paige's card reads *Trapeze Artist*. Cassie and Sophie's cards read *Mystery Author* and *Dancer*. They have to guess what their cards say while you and Riley take turns giving them clues. The team whose members guess correctly with the fewest number of clues will win ten stars.

You can feel your heart beating fast. You really want to do well on this first challenge.

Riley gives Paige the first clue: "You fly through the air with the greatest of ease."

"Trapeze flyer!" Paige shouts.

Riley cheers.

 Turn to
page 51.

"I'll take the back," you say.

Riley hops in the front of the boat, followed by Paige, Cassie, and Sophie. You push off from the shore and are getting ready to climb in yourself. Then you realize that there was nothing in the rules about getting *into* the boat.

You run through the shallow water, pushing the boat forward. Your strategy is definitely working. Riley looks over her shoulder and sees what you're doing.

"I'm going in!" she shouts. She jumps into the water, too.

With Riley in the front and you in the back, you get a huge head start on the other two boats. Your team finishes first! You give each other a round of high fives.

You're proud of your team for winning the challenge, but you're proud of yourself, too, for being brave enough to "take the plunge" and try something new.

The End

You hop in the front of a boat, followed by Cassie, Sophie, and Paige. As soon as Riley hears the whistle, she pushes off and jumps in the back of boat. Then you all start using your hands to paddle like crazy.

Girls on the beach are chanting "Go! Go! Go!" and you're having a blast. You're getting into the rhythm of paddling with your hands, first on the right side of the boat and then on the left. You're concentrating so hard that you barely notice a boat pass yours.

When you look up, you see the Fashionistas in the boat in front of you, only the team members aren't actually *in* the boat. They're in the water! The girls are holding on to the sides of the boat and running through the shallow part of the lake. No wonder they're beating you.

Turn to page 53.

You glance again at Cassie's card: *Mystery Author.* Your mind goes blank. "Um, you type on the computer a lot," you say.

Cassie gives you a blank stare. You're embarrassed about your lame clue.

"About detectives," Riley adds.

"In books," you add.

"Mystery writer?" Cassie asks.

"That's it!" you tell her.

And now it's time for Sophie. Riley rises up on her tiptoes and brings her hands together over her head in a ballerina pose.

"Ballerina!" Sophie says.

You nod like crazy while you do a tap dance.

"Dancer!" she says.

Yes! You worked as a team and finished the challenge using just a few clues.

 Turn to page 54.

You, Paige, and Sophie put on hats. The game leader tells Cassie and Riley to flip over the cards on the front of your hats. You have to guess who you are—or what's on your card—while Cassie and Riley take turns giving you clues.

Paige guesses that she's a swimmer on the very first clue. Sophie needs two clues to guess that she's a famous singer. Then it's your turn.

Cassie turns over the card in your hatband. "You wear a red nose," she says.

You shout the first thing that pops into your head. "A reindeer!"

"You wear a big, fuzzy wig," Riley says.

Your mind is blank.

"You have big, floppy feet," Cassie says.

"A clown," you guess, and you're right!

Riley gives you a high five.

"That was a hard one," she says.

It *was* hard, worrying that you might let your teammates down, but you're proud of yourself for taking a risk and putting on a hat.

CLOWN

Turn to page 54.

Brilliant! you think. There was nothing in the rules about staying in the boat.

You stop paddling and get to your feet. "I'm going in," you shout.

The only problem is that Paige has the same idea. You jump over the same side of the boat at the same time. Before you can even open your mouth to warn your team-mates, the boat tips over, and the others are dumped into the lake, too.

The cold water takes your breath away. When you pop back up and see Paige's shocked, wet face beside you, though, you can't help but laugh. She starts giggling, too, until she notices that *both* of the other boats are in front of yours now.

"Let's get this turned over!" she shouts, reaching for the side of the boat.

The five of you struggle to turn your boat over and finish the challenge. You finally do, coming in last. Everyone else is laughing about your unexpected "swim," but Cassie is clearly angry. There's no question whom she blames for the team's loss—*you.*

 Turn to page 57.

The Curious Cats are next. They get stuck on president of the United States and use one more clue than your team did.

Now you all gather around the Fashionistas.

Shelby's card shows the Statue of Liberty. Zoé poses like Lady Liberty while she and Isabel give clues to Shelby. Maybe it's the pressure of the game, or maybe Zoé's English isn't as good as you thought it was. Whatever the reason, her clues keep falling flat. You can see that even though Shelby is giving her teammate encouraging smiles, Becca and Jamie are getting frustrated.

When Zoé shouts a clue in French instead of English, your teammates—Cassie and Sophie—crack up. Cassie starts imitating Zoé's French accent, and they laugh even harder.

Not nice, you think.

Zoé turns to see where the laughter is coming from and sees you standing in between the giggling girls.

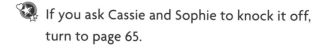 If you ask Cassie and Sophie to knock it off, turn to page 65.

 If you keep quiet, turn to page 56.

You know that laughing at Zoé just because she speaks another language is wrong, but you don't want to mess things up with your new teammates either.

Riley is braver than you are. "How would you like to play this game in a foreign language?" she says to Cassie and Sophie. "Zoé is trying her best."

Cassie frowns. "I was just joking around," she says. "Besides, what's wrong with poking fun at other teams? We're supposed to be rooting for the Shining Stars. Don't you want to win?"

"I want to win," Riley says firmly, "but not by dragging other teams down. I want to win by doing our best."

Cassie backs down, but everyone on your team seems a little uneasy. You hope things go better in the next game: "Row, Row, Row Your Boat."

 Turn to page 46.

"Great job turning the boat over," Cassie says snidely, looking straight at you.

"Hey, I helped," Paige jokes, trying to lighten the mood.

Cassie frowns. "If we had kept paddling, we could have come in second at least," she insists.

Cassie's words sting. Did you let your team down? Then you see Paige pouring water out of her shoe, and when your eyes meet, the two of you start giggling again.

You remember back to the start of the games, when you were so afraid you'd embarrass yourself during a wacky challenge. Getting dumped into the lake *was* a little embarrassing, but it was pretty fun, too.

Riley takes a deep breath. She's about to defend you, but you beat her to it. "The Fashionistas beat us because they had a better idea," you tell Cassie, "not because I turned the boat over. And besides, I think our team came in first in *fun*."

"Agreed," says Paige with a broad smile. Even Sophie grins and nods as she wrings out her soaking wet T-shirt.

You don't know what the rest of the challenges are going to bring, but you've already met a big one. You were brave enough to take some chances and have some fun, and the games have only just begun.

The End

"The first thing we need is a name," Isabel announces when the team gathers in the art studio. "How about the Fashionistas?"

"I'm not that into fashion," Becca says. "What about the Fierce Fighters?"

Isabel wrinkles her nose. "That's kind of extreme," she says.

You think for a minute and suggest the first name that comes to mind. "How about the Big Dreamers?" you ask.

Everyone likes your suggestion, which makes you feel great. Soon you're painting T-shirts and a big banner with your team name splashed across it.

When you finish painting, you suggest that you all head to the student center for a snack, but Zoé has another idea.

"I just got a package from home with some French snacks in it," she says. "Do you all want to come to my room?"

You and your teammates follow Zoé to Brightstar House. You can't believe how quickly she managed to decorate her room, which is filled with pictures from home and a few pillows and posters you recognize from Dream Décor.

Zoé heads to a partially opened box on her desk and pulls out a few containers with French writing on them. You recognize a tube of crackers, but you can't figure out what's in the jar filled with grayish-looking paste.

"Pâté," Zoé announces when she sees you looking at the jar. "And French cheeses, too." She starts to unwrap a block of greenish-looking cheese.

You've heard that French cooking is fancy, but as Zoé arranges the snacks on plates, they don't look fancy at all. And they kind of smell.

"What's pâté?" Isabel asks.

"It's made from liver and vegetables," Zoé answers happily.

Isabel shrugs and gamely spreads some of the gray paste on a cracker. Zoé watches you, waiting for you to try her treats, too.

If you try something, turn to page 60.

If you don't, turn to page 62.

Isabel pops the cracker in her mouth and chews, a frozen smile on her face. She swallows hard.

While Zoé offers you a plate of snacks, you see Jamie over her shoulder, grabbing her own throat like she's been poisoned. Becca makes a disgusted face, too, and then they both start snickering.

Zoé gives you a grateful smile when you spread what seems to be the least stinky cheese on a cracker and pop it into your mouth. *Ugh.*

When Zoé turns around to fill her own small plate with snacks, you quickly spit your cheese and cracker into a napkin.

After a few minutes, it's obvious that Becca and Jamie aren't going to try any of Zoé's snacks, and Isabel has had her share, too. Zoé's cheeks turn pink as she starts putting the snacks away.

Finally, Becca gets to her feet. "I'll see you all at the opening ceremony tomorrow," she says. "Jamie and I are going over to Sweet Treats bakery for a cupcake."

Zoé's face falls. You can tell she feels bad, but you don't know what to do.

 Turn to page 69.

Isabel is incredibly nice to try Zoé's pâté, but there's no way you're going to taste that awful gray paste. And the cheeses don't look very appealing to you either.

"Some Brie?" Zoé asks.

It's the least stinky of the cheeses, but there's a white film on top that you think might be mold. You shake your head and mumble that you're not hungry. Behind Zoé's back, Becca plugs her nose, which sends Jamie into a fit of muffled laughter.

Zoé's cheeks turn a bright shade of red.

You can tell that Isabel's about to say something, but Becca jumps to her feet before she can. "I'm heading over to Sweet Treats for a cupcake," she announces. "Anyone want to come?"

Jamie jumps up to join her.

You stay behind with Isabel to try to make Zoé feel better. *Will the Big Dreamers really be able to work as a team?* you wonder. It's not looking good.

 Turn to page 69.

Zoé's right. Your cartwheel was a disaster, but the crowd loved the way you jumped up and laughed at yourself. You don't feel embarrassed anymore. You're kind of proud, actually, and you have Zoé to thank for that. Her courage and willingness to try cartwheels—and other new things—inspired you.

For the rest of the day, instead of being jealous of Zoé, you cheer her on. And her cheers for you are just as loud.

Your team does pretty well in the challenges, but you realize that you failed a big challenge the day before. You were afraid to try something new, and you made Zoé feel bad.

That afternoon, when the games are over, you knock on Zoé's door.

"How about a snack?" you ask. "I think it's about time I tried pâté."

The End

You vote for cartwheels because they're easy for you.

Zoé practices a few shaky cartwheels while Isabel gives her pointers. Zoé's third cartwheel is almost good, but what impresses you even more is how hard she's trying when she didn't even want do a cartwheel in the first place.

On Zoé's fourth try, she falls over sideways, but she pops up laughing, totally ignoring the smirk on Jamie's face.

When the Big Dreamers are announced, Becca does a couple of fabulous cartwheels across the field. Isabel and Jamie follow close behind. You watch as Zoé takes a deep breath and tackles her cartwheel. Her legs aren't straight, but she does it, and you can see that she's proud of herself.

Then the announcer calls your name.

Turn to page 91.

You can see the hurt in Zoé's eyes when she realizes Cassie and Sophie are laughing at her. Now you're feeling more protective of Zoé than jealous.

"Could you win this game in another language?" you ask your giggling teammates. "She's doing her best."

Cassie rolls her eyes. "As long as she does her best for the losing team," she says. But she quiets down after that.

Riley steps up from behind you and whispers, "That was really brave. It takes courage to stand up for friends."

Zoé must have heard you speak up for her, too, because she gives you a grateful smile.

You know now that Logan was right about the games leading to new friends. You're pretty sure you just made one.

The End

It takes courage to stand up for friends.

You vote for leapfrog. Becca and Jamie roll their eyes, but Zoé gives you a relieved smile.

When the announcer calls Isabel's name, she crouches in the grass. Zoé hops over her, followed by Becca, Jamie, and finally you.

After a few other teams are introduced, the announcer calls one girl from each team up to the judges' table to choose the first challenge for her team. You head to the table to represent your team.

You have a choice between tug-of-war and a "Style Scavenger Hunt."

You're not sure you like the sound of the scavenger hunt. Isabel and Zoé know all about style, but you don't. You're afraid you might feel left out again. But will the Big Dreamers win a tug-of-war?

If you choose the Style Scavenger Hunt, turn to page 68.

If you choose tug-of-war, turn to page 78.

You swallowed your fear when you signed up for the Innerstar U Games, but that was different. Student council is way more important, and if you mess up, you'll be letting the whole school down. You can't deal with that right now.

"Between classes and the games and everything else, I don't think I can," you tell Logan.

Logan seems genuinely disappointed. "That's too bad," she says. "Maybe next year."

You find out the next day that because student council is short a member, Logan decided to drop out of the Innerstar U games and focus on student council. The Curious Cats are short a member now, too, and there's talk of the whole team dropping out of the games.

You feel awful. Logan invited you to join the student council because she believed in you and because she *needed* you. You said no because you were afraid of making a mistake and letting her down, but you let her down anyway—because you weren't brave enough to even try.

Next time, you promise yourself, *I'll be brave enough to say yes.*

The End

You choose the scavenger hunt. You may not know a lot about fashion, but your teammates do, and that gives the Big Dreamers a pretty good shot at winning.

Your team will go head-to-head with Logan's team, the Curious Cats. Both teams gather around the judges to hear what the challenge is about.

One judge hands each team a red purse with twenty dollars inside. "Your challenge takes place at the Shopping Square," she says. "Whichever team can put together the most complete outfit in half an hour wins ten stars."

Isabel's blue eyes sparkle. "I'm on this!"

Zoé nods enthusiastically and links arms with Isabel.

The judge blows the whistle, and both teams take off in the direction of the Shopping Square.

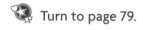 Turn to page 79.

The next morning, the Big Dreamers meet outside the Good Sports Center for the opening ceremony.

Some of the teams are doing wacky stunts across the field when their names are announced. Becca and Jamie want the Big Dreamers to do cartwheels. Zoé confesses she's never done a cartwheel, so Isabel suggests you leap-frog over one another instead.

"Let's vote," Becca says. "I vote for cartwheels."

Jamie raises her hand for cartwheels, too, which is no big surprise. That means it's a tie vote—two to two—and your vote will break the tie.

You prefer cartwheels, but you still feel bad about the pâté incident, so you wonder if you should side with Zoé.

If you vote for cartwheels, turn to page 64.

If you vote for leapfrog, turn to page 66.

The Big Dreamers and the Curious Cats get to the judges' table at the same time. Logan is modeling her team's outfit. It's cute, but her team didn't think to include the red purse.

Zoé, wearing the Big Dreamers' outfit, has more accessories and looks more pulled together. The Big Dreamers win ten stars!

"Woo-hoo!" Isabel cheers.

While Becca and Jamie are busy congratulating each other on their expert spy skills, Zoé compliments Isabel on knowing the market so well.

"Well, we couldn't have done it without you," Isabel says, wrapping an arm around Zoé's shoulder.

Just when you think your teammates have forgotten about you, Isabel turns to you and adds, "Figuring out to include the purse was brilliant. Nice job, teammate!"

You're glad Isabel remembered your contribution. You may not be as stylish as Zoé, but your smart idea helped your team take the win.

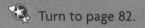 Turn to page 82.

Becca offers to take the position farthest away from the mud. She plays a lot of soccer and has strong legs, which will be a huge help in this challenge. "Let's *win* this," she says.

Jamie stands in front of Becca and grabs the rope. "There's no way I'm getting covered in mud," she says.

Zoé smiles at you nervously. "I'm not so strong," she says.

"Me neither," you tell her. "Let's you and I stay in the middle."

Isabel flexes her arm muscle with a laugh and takes the lead.

The other team is powerful. You struggle to stay in place. Finally, you're able to take a step back, pulling Isabel and Zoé with you. Then Zoé stumbles and lets go of the rope. There's a powerful tug from the other team, and if you don't let go, too, you'll trample her!

"Hold on!" Becca yells.

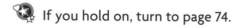 If you hold on, turn to page 74.

If you let go, turn to page 76.

"Maybe we can use the red purse," you suggest. "I bet we can find a red bracelet or necklace that will go great with it."

"Good idea!" Isabel says. "C'mon." She grabs your hand and pulls you to a table full of jewelry and other accessories, including a cute little hat that matches the purse. Isabel pays for the hat while you buy a red bracelet for fifty cents. Then Zoé adds a scarf that pulls it all together.

"You're so good at this!" Isabel says to Zoé. "You should be the one to model our outfit for the judges."

Zoé gives her a big smile before running off to the fitting room at Casual Closet to change her clothes. You're all due back at the judges' table in seven minutes. You hope Zoé is as fast a dresser as she is a stylish one.

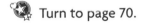 Turn to page 70.

"Watch out!" you yell, holding on to the rope with all your strength.

Zoé rolls out of your way just before you lose your footing and plow into the mud behind Isabel. You slide sideways in the slippery mess. Seconds later, Jamie and Becca fall in behind you.

When Isabel pops up out of the pit and turns around to look at you, you see mud oozing off the end of her nose. That cracks you up. Pretty soon both you and Isabel are laughing so hard, you can barely catch your breath.

"It's *not* funny," Becca sputters, trying to stand up in the mud. "We should have won that." She casts a dark glance backward at Zoé, but Zoé ignores her. She has her sights fixed on a spot in the mud pit just beside Becca.

"Look out below!" Zoé giggles as she leaps into the mud. Then she gathers up a handful of goop and slings it in Jamie's direction.

"Hey!" says Jamie, dodging the mud and scooping up more mud balls to fling back at Zoé. When one of those blobs hits Becca squarely in the face, you hold your breath, waiting for her to start yelling.

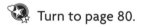 Turn to page 80.

"Woo-hoo!" Isabel yells, giving you and Zoé high fives. "Great teamwork."

"Ten stars!" Becca yells, pumping her fist in the air.

You're excited, too, but as your team celebrates, you notice that the other team is laughing and cheering even more loudly as they roll around in the goop.

"Losing actually looks like more fun than winning," Zoé says, taking the words right out of your mouth.

"I know," you say, and then—before you can even think it through—you say, "Let's go!"

You dive into the mud, with Zoé and Isabel on your heels. Jamie shrugs and jumps in, too.

Becca is standing on the side, watching you like you're all crazy. The next thing you know, she dives in, too. You're all in the mud together and having a blast!

Diving in was the right thing to do, you think. *Diving into the mud pit*—and *diving into the games.*

The End

You let go of the rope. Sure, you've been a little jealous of Zoé, but that doesn't mean you're willing to trample her in order to win.

Jamie gets pulled forward, and soon she's right on Isabel's heels. Your teammates are trying really hard to stay out of the mud, but now it's three against five.

"Go to the back!" Becca yells.

You don't know what she means, but Zoé gets it right away.

She runs behind Becca and grabs the rope. Then you do too. Together, you're able to pull your teammates back away from the pit, and pretty soon, the other team is covered in mud.

The Big Dreamers win!

 Turn to page 75.

You don't say anything about the purse. Isabel and Zoé are the ones who know all about fashion. You figure that if including the purse were a good idea, they would have thought of it already.

Your team gathers a couple of inexpensive accessories at the Market, and then Isabel asks Zoé to be the one to model the outfit for the judges. When you get to the judges' table, you see Logan wearing the Curious Cats' outfit. You do a quick mental count of the number of pieces in her outfit, and your heart sinks. Logan is wearing just *one* more item than Zoé. The Cats win ten stars, and your team earns only five.

"We wondered if the teams would think of using the red purse as an accessory," one of the judges says. "Neither one of you did."

Isabel smacks her palm against her forehead. "I totally forgot about the purse," she groans.

You know that with Isabel's expert fashion skills, the Big Dreamers could have won this challenge—if only you had opened your mouth. You passed up a chance to help your team because you decided your ideas just weren't good enough.

The next time I have an idea, you tell yourself, *I'll be brave enough to share it—no matter what.*

The End

"Which one are you doing?" Logan asks as she steps up to the table behind you.

You think about it for a moment and then say, "I've got some good athletes on my team. I'm going for the tug-of-war."

"Fun!" Logan says with a smile. "And good luck. Tell Zoé I'm rooting for her."

Zoé again. Isn't Logan rooting for *you*, too?

You thought tug-of-war would be a fun, easy way to start the games, but as you and your team approach the tug-of-war pit, your stomach starts doing flip-flops. The judge quickly explains the rules, which are simple: the team that stays out of the goop wins!

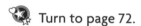 Turn to page 72.

Isabel and Zoé plan a strategy: they decide to run to the secondhand store in the basement of Casual Closet to put together an inexpensive outfit. Then they'll head to the Market, a cluster of tents on the edge of the Shopping Square, where they can find some fun accessories.

Becca and Jamie decide to spy on the Curious Cats and to report back in fifteen minutes on the other team's progress.

As for you? You feel useless. You watch Isabel and Zoé run from rack to rack at Casual Closet, wishing you had as much fashion sense as they do.

Isabel finds a striped top for five dollars. Zoé pairs it with a cute little skirt. Then Isabel adds a pair of boots.

Isabel pays for everything, and you head for the tents in the Market, where Becca meets you with a full report. "The Curious Cats already have a hat and a necklace," she says.

"We need accessories!" Isabel says. "But we're running out of money."

If you point out that she can use the red purse as an accessory, turn to page 73.

If you stay quiet, fearing the others will think your idea is silly, turn to page 77.

To your surprise, Becca starts laughing, too. She throws a giant wad of mud at Jamie, which misses her and hits you instead.

"I think brown is really more *your* color," you joke, flinging goop back in Becca's direction.

You're all having so much fun that you barely notice when the winning team jumps in with you. They've earned ten stars for winning, but the judges award the Big Dreamers five stars for being good sports and for having fun.

You remember back to the start of the games, when you were so worried about making a fool of yourself. You probably do look a little foolish, sitting here covered in mud, but who cares? Your new friend Zoé is sitting beside you, laughing at herself, too.

Maybe I don't have to be afraid of embarrassing myself, you think. *Maybe I can be brave like Zoé.*

The End

Over lunch, the student center is full of girls chattering excitedly about the morning's events. Some teams took part in boat races. Others played guessing games.

After lunch, you're ready for your next challenge. Your team heads to the sports center, where you're faced with a riddle:

Humans or horses?
Take your pick.
You'll need one or the other
For your next trick!

If you choose humans, turn to page 84.

If you choose horses, turn to page 85.

Isabel opens her mouth to defend Zoé, but you surprise yourself by speaking up first. You're a little afraid of how Becca will react. She can be pretty harsh, but you can't let her get away with being so rude to a teammate.

"How was Zoé supposed to know we use a different set of measurements, Becca?" you say. "You're being totally unfair."

"That's right," Isabel says, backing you up.

Becca looks to Jamie for support, but even Jamie looks away.

Now Becca seems embarrassed. "I'm sorry," she mumbles.

Braving Becca's anger was easier than you thought it would be. Speaking up for Zoé was the right thing to do, and as soon as you've done it, you feel your jealousy toward her fade away.

You're ready to get to know Zoé better, and her grateful smile lets you know that she feels the same way. Whatever happens in the games, you realize that you've already won—a new friend.

The End

★ 84 ★

You choose humans (because you know a lot more
about humans than you do about horses), and your teammates agree. But then you learn that the challenge will take
place at Pet-Palooza, which leaves you wondering what
wacky contest the judges have come up with.

When you get to the pet day-care center, you learn that
you and your teammates will be doing an obstacle course.
One of the Big Dreamers will be blindfolded and have a
leash attached to her wrist while the rest of you guide her
through one of the obstacle courses used to train puppies.

You've spent some time with the pups at Pet-Palooza,
but you've never led a puppy, let alone a human, through
an obstacle course. You're relieved when Zoé volunteers to
be blindfolded. She's so brave!

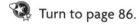 Turn to page 86.

Your team agrees to choose horses. You, Isabel, and Jamie have all ridden the horses at Rising Star Stables. Becca is an experienced rider, and Zoé says that she rode horses all the time back home, too.

When you get to the stables, you look for Silver Sky, Fleet, and your other favorite horses. Instead, you see a few wooden sawhorses set up with hobbyhorse heads. You and Isabel exchange a curious glance.

The riding instructor quickly explains your challenge. One of you has to saddle the sawhorse—blindfolded—while the rest of you give her instructions.

"Sounds simple enough," says Becca. "We can win this!"

Becca volunteers to wear the blindfold and saddle the horse, and Zoé will take the lead on giving her instructions.

 Turn to page 88.

Isabel slips Zoé's blindfold over her eyes while you attach the leash to her wrist.

"Ready?" you ask.

"Ready," Zoé says brightly.

The judge sets her stopwatch and says, "Begin."

You, Isabel, Becca, and Jamie walk alongside the course, giving Zoé instructions as she goes.

"Walk forward three feet," you say, tugging gently on the leash to guide her.

Zoé takes three big steps forward, but that's not the same as three feet.

"No, go back a foot," Isabel says. "Twelve inches."

Zoé hesitates and then takes a small step backward. She seems confused.

 Turn to page 89.

Becca's confidence doesn't last long. Saddling a fake horse blindfolded is a lot different from saddling a real one with your eyes open. First, she puts the saddle on backward. Then she fumbles with the bridle, which goes over the hobbyhorse head.

Zoé might be an expert with horses, but she suddenly realizes that she's not an expert at the English words for the parts of a bridle. When she can't think of the word *noseband*, Becca gets frustrated.

"Hurry up!" she shouts at Zoé.

The riding instructor interrupts to say that if Becca had been saddling a *real* horse, she would have frightened it into trotting off with the saddle only half on. Becca quiets down after that, but the Big Dreamers still come in third behind the Curious Cats and a team called the Starlights. When she hears the news, Becca storms out of the stable, with Jamie close behind.

Zoé seems really upset, too. You feel like you should say something to make her feel better, but Isabel steps up and puts her arm around Zoé before you get the chance. You're not even sure that they notice when you leave.

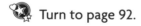 Turn to page 92.

"Take another step backward and then step sideways about two feet," you say.

Once again, Zoé seems confused. "Meters," she says. "What's that in meters?"

"Oh no!" Becca says. "She's on the metric system!"

While you try to remember what feet and inches equal in the metric system, Jamie shouts the same instructions over and over again—as if Zoé will magically understand if she hears the words enough times.

Other teams reach the finish line long before Zoé does. Her eyes are full of tears when she pulls off her blindfold. She tries to apologize, but Becca cuts her off.

"You should have told us you don't understand measurements," she snaps.

 If you defend Zoé, turn to page 83.

 If you say nothing, turn to page 90.

You think Becca's being unfair, but you don't want to bring her sharp tongue down on you, so you keep quiet.

Isabel doesn't share your fear. She steps right up to Becca and tells her to knock if off.

"The rest of the world uses the metric system, Becca," Isabel says. "Zoé did her best. You should thank her for being brave enough to try."

Becca stares at Isabel for a moment and then finally grumbles an apology to Zoé. It doesn't sound very sincere to you, but Zoé is polite, of course. She tells Becca not to worry about it.

As the five of you walk back toward Brightstar House, tension hangs in the air like a thick fog. The Big Dreamers are starting to feel more like the Big Nightmares. Will you be able to pull it together and compete as a team?

 Turn to page 92.

You've been so focused on Zoé that you're caught off guard when you hear your name. You take off too quickly on your cartwheel. Your arm buckles beneath you, and you crumple to the grass—in front of the *entire school.*

Suddenly you're surrounded by silence. You're tempted to roll over and hide your face in the grass, but then you remember how Zoé popped up and laughed at herself. You do the same, waving to the girls in the stands with a big grin. You're rewarded with a huge cheer.

While the next team is being introduced, Isabel and Zoé jog over to you to make sure you didn't get hurt.

"Just my pride," you joke. "That was embarrassing."

"But it was pretty brave," says Isabel. "You weren't afraid to laugh at yourself."

"And the crowd loved it!" Zoé adds with a smile.

Turn to page 63.

A brave girl isn't afraid to laugh at herself.

That evening after dinner, you walk back to your room feeling totally exhausted. You're glad the day is over and that the games are on hold until next Saturday. That'll give your team a chance to bond over the next few days and hopefully patch up some of the hurt feelings.

When you get to Brightstar House, you see Logan at the end of the hall near your room—and Zoé's. You're sure she's there to see Zoé.

"Hi," Logan says with a bright smile. "I have a question for you."

"I don't know where Zoé is," you say with a sigh. "She might still be at dinner."

Logan's forehead wrinkles with confusion. "I'm here to see *you*," she says. "One of the girls had to drop out of student council. Can you take her place?"

"Me?" you ask. "On student council?" You don't know what to say. You've honestly never thought about it.

"You'd be perfect," Logan says encouragingly.

Logan's invite makes you feel good. Now you're really glad that you didn't spill your jealous feelings about Zoé all over her. She was thinking of you all along.

"Wait, don't I have to be elected?" you ask.

"Not this time," says Logan. "This is a special case, because someone had to leave. But you could run next time. You'd definitely get elected."

You think about her offer for a moment. Being on student council could be exciting. You'd be a part of making Innerstar U—a great school—even greater.

Logan sure seems confident in your abilities, but is she right? Could you be a good student council representative?

Aside from Logan, you don't know any girls in student government. What if you don't fit in? What if you don't know what you're doing? Making mistakes in front of a bunch of strangers would be awful, especially since you'd be letting Logan down, too.

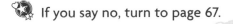 If you say yes anyway, turn to page 94.

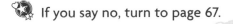 If you say no, turn to page 67.

You're a little scared, but you're excited to spend time with Logan again. You decide to go for it. "I'd love to be on student council," you say.

"Yay!" Logan says, giving you a big hug. "Our next meeting is on Tuesday. I'll see you there!"

A few days later, you're at the student center sitting in on your first meeting. Logan introduces you to everyone, and then starts the meeting. Everyone starts talking so fast about projects and fund-raisers that your head is spinning. It feels like they're speaking a different language.

Being the new girl in a group is hard, you realize. You wish you had friends in the room, but the only girl you know— Logan—is too busy running the meeting to make you feel at home.

It suddenly occurs to you that this must be how Zoé feels sometimes. Maybe you should reach out to her and really try to get to know her.

If you invite Zoé to do something with you, turn to page 98.

If you decide that enough of your friends are already giving Zoé special attention, turn to page 96.

After the student council meeting, you head back to your room. You promised Shelby and Isabel that you'd go with them to a movie that's playing at U-Shine Hall tonight.

You knock on Shelby's door and Isabel's, but there's no answer. Finally you walk over to U-Shine Hall by yourself. Shelby waves from a seat in the auditorium just as the lights go down. Zoé and Isabel are on either side of her, but there's no empty seat for you.

You slip into the back row by yourself, feeling awkward and out of place.

As the movie starts, you notice that Logan and the rest of the student council are sitting together, too, a few rows behind Shelby. Now you feel left out by *two* groups. You barely even see the rest of the movie. You're too busy deciding that no one likes you anymore.

🌟 If you tell your friends how you feel, turn to page 99.

🌟 If you say nothing, turn to page 100.

Zoé looks upset when she opens her door, and when you ask if she wants to walk to the meeting together, she bursts into tears.

"I'm not going to the meeting," Zoé says. "No one wants me on the team. Isabel is too nice to say so, but I know it's true. And I can't blame you. We lost that last challenge because of me."

You're stunned. You don't blame Zoé for your losses, but when Becca did, you didn't defend Zoé. Now you know that by saying nothing, you were letting Zoé believe that what Becca said was true.

"I'm sorry," you say gently. "I didn't blame you, Zoé. I was just afraid to stand up to Becca."

Zoé blows her nose and nods. "I know. I'm kind of afraid of her, too," she admits with a half-smile.

For some reason, Zoé's confession gives you courage. "Maybe we can help each other stand up to Becca," you suggest. "I'll try to be brave if you will. Deal?"

This time, Zoé's smile spreads across her whole face. "Okay," she says, wiping her eyes. "I'll try."

As the two of you head upstairs, you're already feeling braver. Having a friend at your side gives you all the courage you need.

The End

After the meeting, you knock on Zoé's door. When she answers, you can tell that she's been crying.

"What's wrong?" you ask. "Can I help?"

Zoé shakes her head. "It's just hard to be so far from home," she says.

You hadn't thought of that. You can go home for the weekend whenever you want, but Zoé lives all the way across the ocean.

You try to think of a way to make her feel better. "There's a movie at U-Shine Hall tonight," you suggest. "Want to go with me?"

Zoé's tears are quickly replaced with a smile. *"Merci,"* she says. "I'd like that."

On your way to the movie, you discover that you and Zoé like a lot of the same things, from movies to music to warm cookies on rainy afternoons. And that gives you another idea.

"Maybe you can come home with me the next time I go," you say. "My family would really like meeting you."

Zoé's smile is all the answer you need.

The End

Telling your friends how you feel is a little scary, but what else can you do? You can't stand feeling this way for a second longer. Maybe talking with your friends will help.

After the movie, you walk up to Shelby. You're relieved to see that Isabel and Zoé have their backs turned and are talking to some other friends. It would be hard to say what you have to say to all three of them at once.

"Hey, how're you doing?" Shelby asks.

"Actually," you say, "I'm not doing very well. Something's really bothering me."

"What is it?" Shelby asks, suddenly all ears. She's always been a great listener, which makes it easier for you to tell her the truth.

You plunge right in. "It just feels like no one remembers I exist anymore," you say. "When I walked into the movie and saw you all sitting together—without me—I felt totally left out."

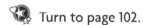 Turn to page 102.

After the movie, you walk back to your room feeling so lonely that you hardly notice the beautiful sunset. You're fighting back tears when Logan runs up behind you. You blink them away before she can see them.

"I'm so sorry," she says. "We were so busy in the meeting that we forgot to tell you about our movie plan."

You force a smile. "No worries," you say to Logan. Her apology makes you feel a little bit better.

Still, though, you don't like the idea of being forgotten. What should you do?

If you vow to become the student council's most unforgettable member, go online to innerstarU.com/secret and enter this code: BBRAVEBU

If you put student council out of your mind for now, turn to page 103.

Shelby's face softens. "I'm sorry," she says. "I knocked on your door before we left, and I saved you a seat."

You let out a huge sigh of relief. "You did?" you ask.

Shelby nods. "Then I saw the student council was sitting together and I thought you'd sit with them," she explains. "So I gave the empty seat to Zoé."

You shake your head with a laugh. You let your jealous feelings about Zoé take over and convince you of things that just aren't true. The girls on student council probably didn't mean to leave you out any more than Shelby did.

You feel a little silly, but you're glad you worked up the courage to ask. Next time, you'll do that *before* you overreact.

The End

It's time to focus on the Big Dreamers. After all, the weekend games are coming, and it'll be time to compete again. Can you pull it together and act like a team? Becca must be wondering the same thing, because she leaves a note on your door inviting you to a team meeting tomorrow in the attic.

After classes the next day, you head up to the attic. As you pass Zoé's door, you wonder if you should invite her to go with you. Becca was pretty hard on Zoé after the last challenge, and you didn't exactly defend her. She could probably use a friend at this meeting.

If you knock on Zoé's door, turn to page 97.

If you head straight upstairs, turn to page 109.

Big Dreamers!
Let's meet in the
attic tomorrow at
3:00. -Becca

"Pillow fight!" you shout, grabbing another pillow from
the couch and playfully bouncing it off Becca's head.

Isabel does the same to Jamie, and soon everyone is
laughing and jumping around in an all-out pillow fight.
Even Becca's having a good time. Before you know it, you're
all in a pile on the floor, laughing hysterically.

"Okay, *okay*," Becca says. "We're the wackiest team.
Maybe we should change our name to the Wacky
Dreamers."

Seeing Becca lighten up a little makes you wish you had been brave enough to speak up sooner.

"Great idea," you say with a giggle. "The Wacky Dreamers it is!"

The End

Becca said she was a fast runner, so Balloon Races seem like a good idea. You're relieved when she agrees. Still, you can't shake the nervous feeling in the pit of your stomach. One look at Zoé's face tells you that she feels it, too.

Things get worse when you hear the race instructions. You have to run a relay race with a *water balloon* between your knees. If you pop the balloon, not only will you get all wet, but you also have to start all over again.

The race should be fun, but you're worrying about Becca's reaction if you pop the balloon or run too slow.

You run the first leg, hoping to just get it over with. You take about three steps before you drop the balloon. *Splash!* Your sneakers are soaking wet. You go back for a new balloon, and this time, you run more slowly. You make it all the way to Isabel without popping the balloon.

Isabel and Jamie catch on that they have to move carefully if they're going to hold on to the balloon. The Big Dreamers are in the lead when Jamie passes the balloon to Zoé, and soon the balloon is between Becca's knees.

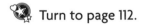 Turn to page 112.

You're afraid of Becca's sharp tongue, but you speak up anyway. "The games are supposed to be wacky and fun, remember?" you say. "Let's not take the fun out of them."

Isabel agrees. Even Jamie, who has been Becca's pal throughout the games, nods her head. Zoé seems relieved.

Now it's Becca's turn to look a little embarrassed. "I'm sorry," she says. "Sometimes I push too hard, but I like to compete—and I like to win."

"What if we compete to have the most fun?" you say.

"Yay!" Isabel says. "We'll be the wackiest team."

Zoé gives you a grateful smile, but Becca isn't convinced. "I don't *want* to be the wackiest team," she says. "I'd still like to win." She stares at the floor.

You notice that Isabel has picked up a soft, pink pillow from the couch and is bouncing it from hand to hand. She gives you a sly smile. You know just what she's thinking.

 Turn to page 104.

You spend the rest of the meeting in a daze. You knew Becca blamed Zoé for some of your losses, but you didn't realize she blamed you, too. You're tempted to quit the team, but that wouldn't be fair to everyone else. You try to pay attention while Becca talks about what the upcoming challenges might be.

On Saturday, you head to the Good Sports Center with your teammates and hope for the best. The two teams that have the most stars at the end of the day will go on to tomorrow's final wacky challenge.

When you and your teammates get to the judges' table to choose your first event, you find that you have to decide between balloon races and something called "Name That Secret."

 If you vote for balloon races, turn to page 106.

 If you vote for "Name That Secret," turn to page 111.

The attic is a cool hangout space on the top floor of Brightstar House. It used to be full of dusty old boxes, but a few months ago, the school cleaned it out. You and your friends worked together to paint the room and decorate it.

Now it's sunny and cheerful, with comfy chairs and couches, bright pillows, a table for studying and doing crafts, and even a mural painted in Innerstar U colors.

Zoé arrives at the meeting just after you do. She seems a little nervous, and you don't blame her. Becca's been kind of harsh. In fact, you're feeling a little nervous, too, about how this meeting is going to go. And the look on Becca's face doesn't exactly calm you down.

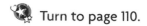 Turn to page 110.

Becca gets right down to business. "I've been going over the results of last weekend's challenges," she says, "and there are only a couple of teams with more stars than us. We can still win this—if we play smart."

Becca looks at Zoé when she says that, and you see Zoé's cheeks starting to turn pink.

"Let's talk about what each of us is best at," Becca says, "so we can choose the right events—events we can win."

Now she's eyeing you. Is she blaming you for choosing the wrong events?

You're tired of Becca blaming everyone else for the team's losses and pushing, pushing, pushing for a win. She's taking all the fun out of the games for you, and you wonder if your teammates feel the same way.

 If you speak up, turn to page 107.

 If you don't, turn to page 108.

The only thing you know about "Name That Secret" is that the challenge will be held at Sweet Treats bakery.

"Maybe it's a cookie-eating contest," Jamie says, patting her stomach. "I can pack away a lot of those."

You all laugh. You hope the challenge is that simple, but you think it'll be something more wacky—and it is. "Name That Secret" is really "Name That Secret Ingredient." You're given a plate of cupcakes, each one with a different secret ingredient in the center. The first team to guess all the secret fillings will earn ten stars.

The first three fillings are easy: marshmallow, peanut butter, and strawberry jam. The fourth one has you all stumped—that is, until Zoé takes a bite. "Cheese," she says. "Ricotta cheese."

"Are you sure?" Jamie asks.

Zoé takes another bite and nods. "Absolutely," she says.

Becca isn't convinced, but Zoé looks her right in the eye. "I'm sure," she says firmly.

 If you support Zoé, turn to page 114.

 If you stay quiet, turn to page 115.

Becca's a fast runner, but that's not the way to win this race. She pops balloons over and over again trying to run fast. She quickly loses your team's lead—and the race.

Becca hangs her head and kicks at the grass just beyond the finish line. *She's as hard on herself as she is on other people,* you think. You'd like to say something to make her feel better, but you're afraid of her reaction.

Zoé's braver than you. "You did your best," she says gently to Becca.

Becca frowns, but she seems to appreciate Zoé's words. That gives you the courage to speak up, too.

"Don't beat yourself up," you say. "It's hard to run *slow* when you're racing to win."

You brace yourself for Becca to snap at you, but instead, she agrees. "I was too focused on winning," she admits. "The girls who slowed down and had fun had the best times in the end."

Then Becca really shocks you. "Thanks," she says to you and to Zoé, "for being great teammates."

Wow, you think. You didn't stand up to Becca when she was being hard on her teammates, but you stood *beside* her when she was being hard on herself. Now, because you were brave enough to follow's Zoé's lead, you'll have a stronger team—and maybe even a new friend.

The End

"If you get this wrong," Becca reminds Zoé, "we all lose."

"If *we* get this wrong," you say pointedly. You're nervous for Zoé because she'll have to face Becca's wrath if she's wrong. But Zoé says she's certain. Shouldn't that be enough reason to support her?

Becca shrugs. "I guess Zoé does know more about cheese than the rest of us," she admits.

Your confidence in Zoé pays off. When the judge says that the secret ingredient *is* ricotta cheese, you all pull Zoé into a group hug. The Big Dreamers win the event and a spot in tomorrow's final challenge.

You walk away from the bakery feeling as if you've learned something. You were so busy being jealous of Zoé that you didn't get to know her. Today, her bravery inspired you to be brave, too, and now you can't wait to find out about her other good qualities. Maybe some of them will rub off on you!

The End

Zoé and Isabel seem to be facing off against Becca and Jamie. That puts you in the middle, and everyone wants to know what you think. It's a tense situation. If you win this challenge, the Big Dreamers will go on to the finals. If not, you'll be cheering for other teams from the stands.

"Zoé seems sure," you say weakly.

"What do *you* think?" Becca asks. "Remember, if you're wrong, we lose."

You take another bite of the cupcake. The filling is sweet, smooth, and *maybe* a little cheesy, but you can't tell. You shrug, just before the judge blows her whistle. None of the teams makes a guess.

"Since no one guessed the last ingredient correctly, both teams will be going on to the final challenge," the judge announces. "The right answer was . . . ricotta cheese!"

 Turn to page 116.

Zoé is much too nice to say "I told you so," but you're sorry that you didn't speak up and support her. As your team leaves the bakery, you apologize.

"I should have trusted you when you said you were sure," you tell Zoé.

"Me, too," Jamie pipes up from behind you.

Zoé shakes her head. "No worries," she says. "We're still going to the final challenge."

Becca is walking beside Jamie. There's an awkward silence while you all wait for Becca to apologize, but she doesn't. Instead, she says, "We've got to shake off this loss. We need to walk into the Good Sports Center tomorrow feeling like winners!"

You're not sure you *can* win—not if Becca doesn't trust her teammates. Should you bring that up now, this late in the games?

 If you stop to talk to Becca about it, turn to page 119.

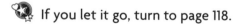 If you let it go, turn to page 118.

Once again, you're impressed with how brave Zoé has been in getting to know new people. Becca is impressed with Zoé, too, especially when Zoé correctly answers questions about Becca's favorite sport (soccer) and favorite color (green).

"How'd you know *that*?" Becca asks, looking surprised but also a little pleased. She suddenly looks like a different person—a much more open and friendly person—which reminds you how little you really know about her.

You're glad the Big Dreamers made it this far, and you still want to win, but now you have another goal, too: to follow Zoé's example and be brave enough to really get to know other people—both new friends and old.

The End

It seems useless to confront Becca this late in the games, so you let it go.

The next day, what seems like the whole school turns out to see the final challenge between the Big Dreamers, the Curious Cats, and another team called the Lightning Bolts. Becca pumps her arms like a champion while Isabel and Jamie wave to the crowd.

The final challenge turns out to be a trivia contest—to test your knowledge about your teammates! You know Isabel pretty well, but you've only just gotten to know Zoé. And Becca and Jamie? You've been classmates with them for a while now, but you haven't hung out very often as friends. You're afraid that might hurt you in this contest.

Sure enough, you flub on a question about Jamie. Then Becca bombs on a question about Zoé. Isabel is the only member of the Big Dreamers who can answer all the questions asked of her, but you're surprised by how much Zoé knows about you and your teammates. She hasn't been at Innerstar U for very long, but she's definitely been paying attention.

 Turn to page 117.

You stop walking and face Becca. You've let too many of her nasty comments slide, and you're tired of the fact that she always thinks she knows best.

"We'd be closer to winning if you had trusted Zoé," you say, trying to keep your voice steady. "Let's agree that the next time one of our teammates says she's *sure*, we have faith in her."

Becca frowns and looks away. She shrugs but finally says, "Okay."

Isabel and Zoé catch your eye and smile as you start walking again, and that makes you feel like a winner. You wish you had spoken up to Becca sooner, but at least you were brave *today*. That gives you the confidence that you can face whatever challenges come your way tomorrow.

The End

Be brave!
Try a few French words:

bonjour *(bohn-zhoor)*: hello, good day,
or good morning
merci *(mehr-see)*: thank you
oui *(wee)*: yes